Thanks

My gracious thanks go to everyone who helped put this book together, including editing, proofreading and so much more. Thank you especially to every reader who has spent time and good money to purchase and read my work, it is you that keeps driving and striving on to do bigger and greater things.

Thank you to all my unwavering friends than continue to encourage and inspire me.

Thank you to my beautiful wife Micki, without whom, I would not be who I am and where I am today. My inspiration, my encouragement, my hope and my flesh muse. I couldn't do any of this with her unshakeable belief and support of me and my passion.

Finally, and importantly thank you to the die hard Freakpeeps out there, that support, encourage and drive me on with begs for more work. For their constant sharing of my work and the message of Freakpeepery and the twisted word. Without whom, I could not spread the word as wide and with as much amusement.

Foreword

Sometimes the best place for inspiration and to use it at its best is when you are at work. Sometimes the workplace is the only place that seems to offer the only inspiration for a tale.

The sights, the smells, the people, the “life” simply happening around you, as though you are inside it, a part of its cycle, yet apart from it, distant while in the centre of its whirlwind.

Watching, listening, absorbing everything. Sometimes we need a story too close to home to shake us up and remind us that flesh is fleeting and the people we see everyday may be the strangest and most distant people of all.

Although this book isn't designed to terrify you into never stepping foot into another building higher than two floors again, I hope it does make you wonder just who you think you know well and who you tell things to.

Hopefully you will see things in beautifully sinister new light and cherish the inventiveness of the human mind when it comes to ways to hurt each other. My only advice? In this case, make sure you don't have any dirty little secrets that maybe larger than you are, or else, someone may just spot the skeletons in your closets and use them against you with wonderfully evil ingenuity.

Stay sick, stay twisted and be freaky my friends.

Rob Shepherd

The Caretaker

Adrian and Monica pulled up and parked in the available space in front of the building. Given the level of cars in relation to spaces available, it seemed like a lucky chance that they found a space at all, let alone one so close to the building itself. They both got out of the car, an 2008 Ford Fiesta.

Not an especially old car, but was still beginning to show some age and wear and tear, patches of rust just creeping in on the cars body in strategic places, like the boot seal and roof line. Adrian was just glad that it hadn't appeared near the wheel arches yet. A new car was most definitely not a realistic option these days.

Adrian sighed heavily as he locked the car, turning to meet Monica, her back to him, now facing the building. Looking up and down at it, the big stone-clad building stood there as a mark of the 60's rush to house the stretching population, convincing the public that the future lay in living in the clouds than in the old houses that had lasted for so long already.

Now, ironically, it was these skyward buildings that were showing their age instead. The once old fashioned houses are now seen once again as a status to be achieved, a measure of moving up in the world, nostalgia of the old streets and old ways driving up their prices. Prices that Adrian knew that he and Monica never be able to earn close to.

The grey and stained building stood there in front of them, tall and imposing. Dominant over it's surroundings. It may have been old, but it's power to overwhelm and strike nervous awe was yet to weaken and wane. Monica reached out and held Adrian's hand as they walked together towards the strangely nerve inducing building. Both looked at each other with the same look that betrayed their facial lies to each other, that this was likely all that they were going to be able to afford to rent together.

A young girl in her early to mid twenties, holding a black leather business folder that bulged with paperwork, greeted them at the entrance to the building.

“Mr and Mrs Spicer?” The girl greeted them with a broad, gentle smile.

“That's right” Monica spoke up as Adrian stared around at the child's park and the big heavy looking steel door right in front of them.

“Hi, I'm Samantha, we spoke on the phone?”

Monica gritted her teeth at the upward infliction in the girl's voice. If anything could grate on her nerves in a second, that was it. She bit her lip and looked at the girl, smiled and nodded. But she could feel the annoyance dissipating the longer she looked at Samantha.

The girl was nice enough she thought and she had helped them get a chance to view this place which technically they didn't really deserve according to council bureaucracy. She looked pressurised and Monica felt a little bit sorry for her.

'Shall we take a look then?' Samantha said, the upward inflection making itself noticeable once again. Once you heard the first time it was impossible *not* to hear it, Monica thought to herself.

“Sure” Adrian answered returning his attention to the girl once again. He tried sounding enthusiastic, but instead he sounded sarcastic and mockingly and immediately wished he had left Monica to talk.

The three of them entered the building via a little black plastic fob which the girl held to the mosaic wall beside them. One of the small tiles was an odd colour, this was known as the “magic brick”.

In seconds the heavy steel door made a metallic clanking sound and slid carefully open for them to pursue into the building itself. They made their way to the lifts. One was waiting patiently there for them and opened dutifully as the girl (Samantha) pressed the call button. Once all three of them were inside she pressed the button for the 6thth floor.

No more than a few moments later than they had arrived, but in the cramped confines of the lift it had felt much longer. They made their way to flat number 29. Although he knew it was stupid, Adrian felt just a little weird. He shrugged it off as best as he could and carried on listening to the girl as she continued to explain;

“We have a caretaker for this building, he's very good, he takes very good care of the building as you can see, but he unfortunately couldn't attend with us today, but if you do decide to take the place, which I'm sure you will, you will bump into him soon enough, he's always around, taking care of the place”.

Adrian looked around the landing, after all these places were usually a dive, but she wasn't wrong, the place was quiet, very quiet and yes clean, very clean. Oddly clean in fact. All metal objects/surfaces were as shiny as an officers pin badge, the floors seemed to squeak as they had walked across them and the smell of glass cleaner, polish and disinfectant combined to create a strange, sanitised odour that lingered in the air, like in a waiting room of a doctors or some place.

Samantha continued to talk as she unlocked the door to the flat, "We don't get hardly any problems here, or near the block to be honest. There are so much worse places than this, trust me I have had to let properties in much much worse places. We do act upon any nuisance or anti-social behaviour that's brought to our attention but since the caretaker started we have never had a problem so I am told and I don't tend to get any complaints about here. So he must do well. All things considered, you have had a lucky break with this place."

Adrian and Monica looked at each other again, Monica rolled her eyes slyly. Adrian smiled in response. They turned back and started to look around the place. The bathroom was much larger than they had expected, along with the kitchen, both of which, Samantha dutifully explained had only just been fitted with brand new suites. The master bedroom was much larger than they expected, as was the lounge. It was probably large enough to comfortable house the furniture that they had in storage without a problem.

The second bedroom was a bit smaller than they thought it would be, but still a good size all things considered.

Adrian's mind drifted as he looked around, it was clearly obvious that he was paying attention because Samantha turned and engaged Monica back in conversation and explained the finer details of the place and the offers' conditions. After they had finished looking around, Samantha explained that they had been offered first choice. If they wanted it, they could have the keys today.

Monica grabbed Adrian's arm once again, snapping him out of his day dream.

“Well?” Monica asked.

“Well what?” Adrian responded.

This met with Monica's stern eye roll and angry stare with her hands finding their way to her front and being folded like a school teacher. His lack of attention annoyed her.

They were in this together, the least he could do was focus on the situation instead of leaving the shit all down to her as always.

“Well? Do you like it? Do you want to take it or not?”

The annoyance in Monica's voice was evident and unmistakable. And as Adrian noted in stark contrast to the polite charm she had painted on her face for the young girl, this Samantha that was offering it to them.

"Do *you* like it?" Adrian asked back in return.

Monica sighed heavily once again.

"Look, I know it's not fantastic like those yuppy river front flats but we can't afford those and likely never will, we can afford *this,* but when all is said and done, this place does look pretty good overall." Monica reasoned.

"It's bigger than we thought it might be and besides, I don't think we will get another chance any time soon. Do you? I think she has made that pretty clear. Take this, or leave with nothing and no more chances".

"Yeah, you're right sweetie. OK, we'll take it then yeah?" Adrian replied, characteristically of him, partly stating whilst also asking a question looking for guidance to make the final decision.

He never changed, Monica thought. Monica turned back to the girl.

“We'll take it, Samantha” Monica replied to her with every bit of the certainty that Adrian had lacked.

“OK then, I just need to run through some boring details on the forms with you and get you to sign them, there are quite a few these days I am afraid.”

The pair listened carefully and signed each form in turn. Then after tidying up all her paperwork and placing it back into her folder, the young Samantha pulled out the keys and fobs, explaining how they work just to be sure and handed them to the couple saying:

“Well, that's it then, it's all yours, tenancy starts Monday, but you can start moving your things in whenever you like. Here are your keys. I hope you enjoy your new home”.

The young girl smiled and made her way to the door,

“I'll leave you two to it, I'll let myself out, any problems just let me know, or speak to the caretaker when you see him. And you're bound to bump into him, he's *always* around to help”.

Samantha smiled once again as she left, shutting the door, their goodbyes still ringing in the air. She made her way out of the building, the moment she stepped foot out of the door, the enthusiastic expression on her face changed to that of apprehension and fear. A look that seemed to say; “Have I done the right thing?”
“Should I have done that?”
“Should I have said something?”

Samantha knew there was something odd about this place but the fact that it is a building that is not usually on her letting remit, she could only guess as to why. None of the other officers had told her anything bad about the place, about any problems or anything like that. But Samantha knew there was something not right about this place, she could feel it.

She sensed it and she couldn't wait to get away from it and hand the damn thing back to her colleague “Maggie” whose area it was to look after in the first place.

As aesthetically pleasing as they had made this place, with the garden, playground, flowers, washing area, and the rest, nothing could mask that this place just wasn't right. Not right at all. In fact, as far as Samantha was concerned, this place was just plain wrong.

Chapter 2

Adrian & Monica had finally settled in to their new home, the furniture was easily swallowed up, much to their surprise. The décor, a standard issue magnolia, was a bit boring but it was in good condition, and rather than go through the expense of decorating again they had elected to keep it.

Decorating the walls with photographs and a collection of modern abstract art instead. As the days passed they began to feel more and more secure. They still didn't feel settled but they were comfortable and secure.

They hadn't *met* all their neighbours, but they had *seen* them, so they knew who lived in which flat. They had met Sally, who lived opposite at number 27. They had seen the young girl who lived next door in the studio apartment, she came and went like a gust of wind. But they had established that she had a boyfriend that worked at Starbucks, who stayed there with her most weekends.

The people at number 30 weren't the social types it seems as they only ever either saw the backs of them leaving down the stairs or getting into the lift. Which left the people at number 31. They were it seemed to be the local weed warehouse. Far too many visitors just to be a very sociable person.

The mornings now however had begun to repeat themselves, much to Adrian's quiet enjoyment. Every morning would be the same, Monica would have the coffee percolator humming away, giving off the strong aroma of Adrian's favourite blend of Columbian coffee wafting through the air.

Adrian, would settle down to the little breakfast bistro table set that Monica's mother had found for them, opposite Monica and they would have toast, coffee and a cigarette before making their way out to work. Sally would greet them both every morning with a big smile and a "Good Morning!" And every morning Adrian would smile back as Monica wished her a good morning back. 20

But every morning as they made their way down to the car, Adrian would have this unsettled feeling that something was wrong, that there was danger here and he knew something bad was going to happen.

The problem was that he couldn't explain any of this. How could he explain that he didn't know what this danger he felt actually was? Or where it was coming or even going to come from.

How could he explain that there was danger here, yet he knew not what it was, where it was, why it was dangerous and why they were in danger? How could he say he just felt creeped out? What kind of explanation was that?

Adrian elected instead to keep quiet about it, for now, even though that felt just as bad.

Chapter 3

Adrian and Monica made their way to their car, just as they got began to get into the car Adrian noticed something moving inside the window beside the entrance door. A thick net obscured the view through the widow but still gave enough sight for Adrian to make out that the shadow was a figure. The figure of a man moving around in the room inside.

Monica called out to Adrian, snapping him out of his momentary trance.

"Come on, I would like to get to work some time today."

Adrian turned and shook his head, as though trying to clear cobwebs from his mind, then proceeded to unlock the car. He couldn't help his eyes diverting back to the window though as he began to put one leg inside.

"What is it with you? What are you looking at?" Monica asked, her patience was beginning to wear thin.

"Oh nothing, just looking at...." Adrian's words tailed off mid sentence as the effort of completing it was too much.

Monica looked over, following Adrian's gaze.

"It's just the caretaker probably. So what? Let's get to work, *please.*"

Finally Adrian snapped himself away and climbed into the car fully. Buckling up, they made their way out of the car park.

The figure placed the cup back down on the old dusty desk, cluttered with all sorts of things from pencils and pens to knives, screwdrivers and tape. A few glass jars decorated the end of the desk, a yellowish fluid filled them, each holding a mysterious object of one sort or another.

The figure turned and walked over towards the door and bent down. Reaching down they picked up the envelope that had been slipped underneath the door. Opening it, they scanned the contents slipped it into their pocket before turning back. Taking something off the desk, they opened the door and made their way to the lift, their keys hanging in their fingers, jingling with an eeriness in the silence of the building.

The figure made their way up to the 9th floor, their keys swinging, creating that ominous jingle still. As though a signalling the approach of a guard to a prisoner that was about to be heading for capital punishment.

The figure turned and walked up to the front door of the flat. Slowly and methodically they knocked on the door. After a short wait the door opened and a man in his early forties, wearing a close fitting vest and jeans stood in the doorway.

“Yeah? What's up?”

The figure didn't speak, instead he handed the note to the young man, then suddenly as he scanned it, the figure raised his other hand. Inside it, he brandished a steel clip that was normally used for holding the mop heads onto the handles when cleaning the floors, however this one was never likely to be used for such purposes.

Instead it was sharpened to a razor like point at the tip, now appearing more like a giant fish hook rather than a clip for mops. At this point the man looked up just in time to see a flash of light glint of the sharpened steel clip before the figure buried it between his shoulder and neck with ruthless efficiency.

The pain was extreme and so intense that the young man felt the air stumble as he tried to scream, leaving only silence to escape from his open mouth. He reached with both hands desperately trying to pull the steel out from his flesh. The blood now beginning to pump out from his wound and running down his body, staining the vest.

The figure yanked him out of the doorway, the young man bending down in subservience under the pain and pressure while the caretaker casually closed the door to the flat and pulled him out through the fire door into the stairwell.

Down the stairs they went. The figure walked nonchalantly down the steps, clip with the unfortunate man attached and panicking, held behind him like he was simply carrying a large bag of rubbish behind him.

Down they went each flight of stairs, at some point the man had felt his footing give way and he slipped forward. It seemed to make no difference to the figure who carried on without even so much as a turn of the head to acknowledge what had happened. He simply carried on, dragging his pierced, unfortunate victim down head first. The young man's body slapped hard with a wet smack on each step as various parts of his anatomy struck the concrete on the way down, creating further injuries.

Finally they were down at the bottom of the stairs. The energy all but gone from the poor young man, who lay there motionless except to move his bloodied and battered head to look and plead silently with his attacker. The figure looked down at him, still not saying a word he simply looked him over briefly before ripping out the sharpened clip and burying it back into his torso for a better grip. The young man twisted and coiled in agony, but it made little difference, they were moving once again and the figure dragged the broken body of his victim out of the back door and around to the side of the building, where he stopped and raised his other hand.

The keys jangling with more menace and bad intention than the young man could have thought possible before this nightmare had begun. The figure placed a key into the lock and opened the large, thick wooden door, which creaked and puffed dust into his bruised and bloodied face. Further he was dragged, into the dark room.

He could see very little if anything in this room, light was at a premium, yet the figure seemed oblivious and moved without problem. The young man could hear pumps whirring loudly somewhere close by but couldn't tell from which direction. They stopped again as the figure opened another door, it creaked as he moved wide enough to step inside.

Then with complete disregard, the figure dropped the young man where he was, as though he was simply another heavy piece of bulk rubbish to be cleared. Suddenly he could hear the tell tale jangle of heavy chains. The more and more as they moved closer.

Suddenly, with an almighty crash of shearing pain, he felt himself lifted up off the floor and the clip ripped out once more from his prone body. He lifted his head with all the strength he could muster and stared into the face of the devil. As far as he was concerned this was not a person, *it,* was something else from the depths of Hell.

To do this it had to be. The figure stared back at him eye to eye, emotionless. Their piercing blue eyes the only thing left that he could see as he was hoisted up and hung with cold and efficient brutality on to the chains. What seemed like a meat hook burrowed into his back sending excruciating pain down his spine. Then as if to compound his suffering his hands were pulled up and outwards and locked into position on the end of two other chains via hand cuffs which were fixed to the concrete wall.

The figure pulled out a knife from the side pocket of his dusty combat trousers and proceeded to stab into the man's hand. Until he reached the webbing between his fingers, slowly he cut the round the diameter of the finger, the skin opening up, revealing the bone. The man writhed and tried desperately to wrench his hands out of the cuffs and away from this psychopath. Then with a crack he felt the bone break before the sickening sound of a pop as his middle finger came off.

The figure looked up at him hanging there like a sick ode to Christ's suffering, then slid his hand into the man's pocket, placing something inside it.

Taking out the envelope from his own pocket, pulled out a photograph from inside and placed it in the man's right hand facing him. Turning away the figure pulled a cord and a dim light buzzed into life. It lit precious little except for part of the figures face, bathing him in more evil than he already seemed, but crucially, also the photograph. The man could not escape from his situation, but worse than that he realised, he could not escape the picture staring back at him in the photograph. A picture he had long since tried to eliminate from his mind and his life.

The figure seemingly satisfied with his morning's work shut the door and locked it again before exiting the area out into the open closing and locking the big wooden door behind him.

Finally the man found his voice. He screamed, loud, piercing screams of howling pain and desperation. They were so loud that he felt like he had made his own ear drums burst. The sad reality was that no-one in the outside world could hear him. Not above the din of the pumps whirring away loudly.

The figure returned back to the office room, closing the door behind him, he opened the metal cabinet at the far end of the room and hung the steel clip on a make shift hook and closed the cabinet. Then turning to the desk he took an empty jar, reaching down beneath the desk he took a large bottle with no label and poured some of the yellow liquid into the jar.

Placing the bottle back into the cupboard he reached into his pocket and dropped the severed finger, still with ring, emblazoned with a diamond cross, into it. Sealing the jar with a lid, the figure, he moved away and sat down into the old creaky chair.

Reaching down, he pulled out a flask of hot coffee and filled the cup, then leaned back into the chair and lit a cigarette, waiting for the morning rush of parents taking their children to school. The floors outside his office fresh and clean, just waiting for the residents to enjoy and appreciate as they smelt the aroma lingering in the air. Just for them.

Chapter 4

It had been a couple of days since Adrian had actually seen the caretaker, at that time he was but a shadow within the work room as Adrian had looked in whilst climbing into his car that eerie morning.

He hadn't seen him since then, but in fairness he hadn't been looking for him not paying any attention as he came and went each morning to and from work.

However he had a well earned holiday from work to enjoy and he fully intended to make every day of the next two weeks last as long as possible, relaxing at home with his feet up.

This morning he had decided to make the most of the early alarm call of Monica's clock to go for a walk, stopping to pick up a newspaper from the convenience store just up the road on the way back.

Arriving back at the building, he pulled his keys out of his pocket to open the security door, when a builder, covered in dust, , with stains, clearly left over from old jobs almost painted on to his clothes, opened the door to exit, startling Adrian gently. Adrian stepped back to let him out, the man nodded and smiled his thanks in return.

“Blimey, you guys start early these days” Adrian chuckled, attempting small talk.

“Oh yeah, they get us in as early as possible now. 8 O'clock start if we can.” The builder replied his eyebrows raising in an open gesture of criticism of his firm.

“So what have you got on today? Anything easy or interesting?” Adrian continued, hoping not to sound as though he was taking an unhealthy interest. Which in a way he was.

“Oh, we've got a void. Looks like the tenant has done a bunk, they've left everything.”

“What happens to all the stuff when people do a runner?” Adrian asked quizzically. “I always wondered that.”

“It goes to storage. If the tenant doesn't call up and claim it, the council dump it all.” The builder said.

“Seems a bit of a waste. Couldn't they give it to the needy, hostels, shelters, that sort of thing?” Adrian quizzed, surprised at this.

“No, they have to dump it now apparently, something to do with EU regulations and health & safety, in case of infestation I guess. If they know it's infested then they get a special team in to clear it, if not we get the call to clear it out and take it to where they want to hold it before it's dumped.”

The builder had that look about his face that said: 'I shouldn't be telling you any of this, but I don't care'.

“Best be getting on, they don't pay the hour these days” The builder said rolling his eyes. Adrian nodded and said his farewells and continued back up to the flat. Back inside, Adrian closed the door and popped his keys back into the dish beside the telephone that Monica insisted upon him doing and walked into the lounge, knocking his trainers off as he did so.

“Coffee's in the pot darling” Monica shouted from the bedroom. “I'll be back around 5.”

Adrian said nothing, just walked into the kitchen placing the newspaper down on the small drop-leaf dining table and poured out a coffee for himself from the pot. After adding some milk and sugar, he made his way back into the lounge sitting down at the table and opened the paper.

Monica by this time arrived back into the lounge and slid her arms over his shoulders and kissed him on the cheek, before picking up her half finished coffee and taking a sip.

“Any idea you what all that noise was this morning?” Monica asked sweetly.

“Oh yeah, talk about coincidence. Bumped into a sort of builder who's working in one of the other flats, think it's the one that was making all the noise.” Adrian said vaguely.

“And?” Monica urged him for answers.

“It's funny because we move in and as soon as we've moved in, somebody else it seems goes and does a bunk.” Adrian elaborated.

“A bunk?” Monica repeated with a quizzical expression.

“Yeah, they just upped and left, leaving all their stuff there and run off somewhere else.” Adrian explained a bit deeper. “But why would anyone do that? Surely you want to take everything you can?” Monica asked again, trying to grasp the idea.

“They probably haven't paid their rent in ages. That's what mostly happens, I think. Fall behind and instead of suffering being evicted, they do a runner, that way they avoid having to pay up all the missing rent.” Adrian continued

“I think they can demand you pay it all in one go if they catch you, well evict you while you are there, but if they can't find you, you can't pay. Simple as that.” Adrian explained the principal as he knew it thanks to hearing from friends how it was supposedly done.

“Well, at least we have enough to pay the rent without problem, I will not be letting this stuff go begging to some council dump or something. It costs a fortune.” Monica sniffed at the thought.

The figure sat in the chair, a dirty coffee stained cup wrapped in their hands as they listened to the hustled and bustle and the chaotic din of the school run. Children crying, laughing, running around, parents either scolding their kids to do as they are told or for *not* doing as they are told, talking to other parents and fellow neighbours in the block as they make their way outside and off to their respective schools, playgroups, nurseries etc. All too soon, the rush and bustle is over, leaving nothing but silence where but minutes earlier was a cacophony of sound.

Silently the figure sat in the old chair, waiting, the old radio faint in the background to the point where it is hard to distinguish accurately what is being played, much less which station it is.

Then, slowly a shuffling of footsteps outside the workroom door and a yellow post it note attached to some photographs slid its way underneath the door and into the room.

The figure slowly stood up, placed the cup down on the bench and stepped over to where the note lay patiently to be read. The figure then bent down, picked it up and held it in their right hand, holding it there for a few elongated moments before detaching it, pocketing the photographs into their back pocket and retiring to the chair once more, placing their dirty booted feet up on the bench, sticking the note to the seal of the blacked out window and reaching out for the cup again.

After finishing the drink, the figure placed the cup down, the last vestiges of the liquid inside dribbling slowly down the side, staining the cup on its way down. The figure placed their feet back down onto the floor before returning to their feet. After a few sweeps of the room by eyesight, they located a Stanley blade, the handle, looking slightly rusty and warped with well worn edge smoothing the grip. The figure reached out, picked it up and opened a draw underneath the bench, revealing a file and an old paint scraper.

Picking them up, they began to sharpen both blades until the tip glinted beneath the false light of the long tube lamp on the ceiling. Turning their attention back to the note they studied it once more. Again, a simple message contained on it reading: “27. Sodomy. Everything.”

The figure, opened the door and walked out, closing it behind them, keys jangling on their belt, they made their way to the lifts placing the Stanley knife in their side pocket of their trousers and holding on to the scraper in hand.

Pressing the appropriate floor button with their dirty stained finger, they waited silently for the lift to close and travel to the floor. Once there, they turned left and through the fire door, the tools scraping upon the floor as they walked.

Not actually getting anything up. It was clearly a ruse to those who were to be inclined to look carefully, but no-one ever did in this building. That was their biggest problems here.

They either paid too much attention to what other people did, or too little. Both would always be to their detriment in the end. After a few moments there was a click as the lock to a door was unlocked and the latch turned. Then the creak as the door resisted slightly to the efforts of the person on the other side to open it. Just then a middle aged man, slightly portly and with a thinning top of hair appeared in the doorway and out onto the landing floor.

Closing the door with a certain thud, they made no attempt to address the caretaker, kneeling down scraping the floor. In fact it's arguable if they even noticed they were even there. This was to be their 2nd mistake.

The occupant walked towards the lifts, both showing on different floors, neither being anywhere near the floor they were currently on. After shuffling their feet a couple of times they decided that they would take the stairs instead for speed and convenience. This was their third mistake.

The caretaker now stood up, scraper brandished tight in their left hand, walked towards the stairs after the man. Looking back at the door from which the occupant had come from. Number 27.

To live at this address was their first and ultimately worst mistake.

Slowly the figure followed the man down the stairs, allowing the scraper to bounce off each spoke/post of the handrail on the way down. Giving off an eerie, sweet twang that echoed ominously off the walls of the stairwell, this being the message that the man after a few moments realised was a message, a message to him and a none to subtle one.

His time was numbered and he was in no shape to negotiate these steps at speed in order to escape his stalker. He was the target and his enemy was already, locked, loaded and ready to take him out.

But that wasn't to say that Terrance Percival wasn't going to try, he had nothing left to lose after all. And with that he began to rush as fast as he could. Down the stairs he ran, each step coming at him faster than the last. Faster and faster he travelled, the clear and certain structure of the stairway becoming less solid, more fluid and more difficult to ascertain where he needed to be placing his feet with each second of travel.

His eyes becoming blurry with the whizzing past of details, his head dizzy and his legs becoming more wobbly and uncertain beneath him as his feet began to move too fast beneath his body for his mind to co-ordinate efficiently, effectively and safely enough.

With a sudden unexpected movement of one foot as he travelled down the steps he felt his body move in the most uncoordinated manner, his mind realising its mistake, desperately trying to adjust itself whilst simultaneously attempting to brace itself for the inevitable impact of a fall.

Within just a fraction of a second, Terrance was tumbling down the steps afore him, his limbs cracking as his body slapped down upon the cold concrete of each step until he ultimately came to rest in what felt like agonising pain sprawled across the landing halfway between flights of stairs to separate floors above and below him.

Unable to move for the pain and possible disabling injuries, Terrance simply lay there, the pain making his eyes swell with tears.

As Terrance lay there, all he could do was listen to the heavy thump of the footsteps above him, coming down slowly and methodically to meet him where he lay incapacitated. The clink and clank of that metal scraper tapping ominously and threateningly against the metal bars of the handrail as his stalker followed him down to where Terrance had come to rest from his fall.

As his eyes, dizzy and blurred stared upon the steps where his head lay facing, he saw a terrifying sign of two thick, strong and dark legs with heavy, sturdy looking boots tread heavy and determinedly down to meet his fallen face. Slowly they stepped down and over his head stopping aside of him. Terrance tried to turn his head to meet them but his neck hurt and restricted him from doing so.

He closed his eyes for a second, waiting for an inevitable hard blow, but after a second or two of waiting without it happening he opened them again, only to be greeted with a large, strong hand reaching down to his face.

Within a split second it had him by the throat, in a tight, vice like grip, much like he imagined the feeling of a boa constrictor would be around his neck. Then seemingly with ease, he found himself raising up from the floor, much like he was floating like some kind of levitating magician would do in a clever illusion, tricking their audience.

Only this was no illusion and this was no magician with their hand across his closing windpipe.

Before Terrance had any time to think he could see his feet beneath him again, yet they too were floating above the ground upon which he had lain mere moments before in a heaped bundle of catatonic pain.

Before he had time to even glimpse, and that's all it was, of a hand holding some kid of weapon inside it, met his face, the side of the hand landing against his face squarely with such force that he heard much less felt, the bones in his nose, and jaw crack and break, sending a searing pain shooting through his entire face.

His eyes immediately beginning to sting and burn in sympathetic reaction to the pain coursing through the impacted areas of his nose and mouth. He felt his front teeth immediately loosen and begin to drop into his mouth.

He wanted to cry and spit them out but his jaw racked with such pain locked and refused to move, simply holding them inside his cheeks and on his tongue causing even worse discomfort.

Quickly he found himself spinning round, his body twisting with such speed he had no opportunity to see the face of his attacker and ended with his being held still aloft the ground but in a tight headlock. Terrance's chin pushed tight against the bulging, solid muscle of the stranger's biceps.

Terrance's arms and legs dangling like the appendages on a string puppet. The figure then began dragging Terrance's pain racked and limp body down the stairs in this headlock on a terrifying journey that seemed to last forever to arrive at a destination Terrance knew not, yet terrified him all the more for it.The figure made his way down the final flight of steps and out of the back security door.

Turning left and making his way to the side of the building to a discreet wooden door, painted with ancient, flaking white paint, which showed its age along with the cracks appearing all over the door beneath the areas where the paint had flaked away and across areas where it had not.

The wood seemed to be suffering the effects of rot as the corners were splintering glimpsing the darkness of the space and the mysterious terrors that awaited him, which lay behind it.

The figure slid the scraper into a spare pocket on the other side of his trousers and pulling the old rusty keys from off his belt loop, unlocked the door and with one swift wrench, yanked it open with very little fuss, defying the seeming age of the door.

A musty, damp stench rushed out and attacked Terrance's sense of smell despite the destruction of his nose, making his eyes tear up once again.

Once inside, the figure slammed the door closed behind them with a deft back kick of his foot and all went almost entirely black, save for a small yellowish glow of an old square lamp on the ceiling somewhere over the side of where they were stood.

Dragging Terrance along further into the terrible, damp of the darkness, the caretaker swung Terrance around once more, causing his head to swirl with dizziness, making him want to vomit if his mouth would only let him.

Then with both hands the figure wrenched him up in what seemed like mid air, although with this little light, Terrance couldn't be sure of anything at this point.

The only thing he knew was the sudden rush of instant pain in his back as he felt something thick and sharp pierce his back amongst the ample fat that surrounded his spine. His body lurched a little as whoever it was threatened to tear itself out again.

Before his body ripped itself apart off from this giant piercing, the figure moved in again pulling one arm up and locking it in what seemed like a metal shackle, before repeating the same to the other arm.

Now fully shackled and tenderised on what he could only imagine was some kind of hook, Terrance had no choice but to face the next stage of his ordeal in this dank, dark and stinking hidden hovel, hidden from the outside world and likely silent to it as well.

He couldn't scream for help or in pain and desperation, so he resigned himself to weeping on the inside instead. Begging God to save him from suffering his torture for any length of time, to take him quickly. But deep inside he knew, that his God had already forsaken him the moment he had fallen on those steps, what seemed like an age ago now.

Now was the time he knew his ordeal was only just beginning.

The figure walked away from Terrance's hook prone body and bent down in the low light, reaching for something. Then turning, they returned and with a clank upon the floor, Terrance realised it was a bucket. The reality of the situation sunk in and he realised that it was about to get so much worse than he could have ever imagined.

Just over the figures shoulder, Terrance spied a slim, home-made shelf which contained several teasingly, unidentifiable items. The caretaker then reached into his pocket and pulled out the scraper and run it up Terrance's body until he got to the top of his head.

That's when he felt an intense burning sensation rush across and over his head. He tried desperately to stop whatever this lunatic was doing to him but his attempts at wrestling his hands free from their shackles were useless and ineffectual. And within a few seconds afterwards felt something flap onto the side of his head, then the other side.

The figure, then having done enough for the moment stepped back and reclined his hand, the scraper held within catching just enough of the little glow of light to glint enough to reveal fresh fluid blood dripping off the leading corner of the blade.

Placing it down on the home-made shelf after a short inspection, the figure then turned his attention to the Stanley blade, which he duly pulled out of the other pocket of his trousers and studied it intensely before stepping forward once again.

Terrance tried to pull his ailing body away from the now open blade of the box cutter. But to little, if, any effect.

The figure then tore at his shirt, revealing Terrance's bare chest. He couldn't be sure but he definitely felt like this madman was shaking his head in either pity or disappointment.

That's when he closed in and brandishing the blade and with sudden and effective brutality sliced at his chest lopping off his left nipple, catching it on the blade and keeping it there with his thumb.

This time, the pain in his chest now feeling more extreme than the pain in his face, Terrance screamed in agony, his teeth that had been knocked from his gums, dropping out of his mouth with a slurp, inside half congealed blood.

Terrance's screams however did nothing to halt proceedings, instead they seemed to encourage them and the caretaker took to the right side of his chest much the same as he had to Terrance's left and deftly sliced off the right nipple as well, unleashing fresh squeals of agony from Terrance in opposition.

Only to urge this nightmare monster onwards further.

Amongst the tears and wails of pain from his victim, the figure of torture, gave a brief rest to his tortured soul before him and turned to the shelf, placing his acquired tokens into a jar of clear water.

Turning back again the figure looked down inspecting the bucket. Then back up to Terrance's quivering body, already seemingly in shock. Then without any warning, tore at Terrance's trousers, breaking the fly zip and yanking them down to Terrance's ankles.

What greeted him was it seemed both something of slight disgust but also to his agreement.

Slowly, the figure of this psychopath masquerading as a caretaker, as Terrance declared him to have to be, raised his left hand and slowly lowered it slightly and ripped down Terrance's worn and sorry looking underpants.

Then, once done, the horrifying character rose his left hand once more, once more lowering it down, this time to meet Terrance's surprisingly solid and erect manhood, standing strangely proud to attention.

Once there he slowly stroked it with what seemed love and careful attention. Over and over again, gentle stroking it with what one could almost interpret as love and maybe even affection.

Terrance forgot himself in this weird, terrifying state of exaggerated excitement and began to groan slightly with a certain amount of twisted, sadomasochistic pleasure, this sensation of almost utter delirious, erotic pleasure.

Just as Terrance felt he was about to explode with pleasure and cover his torturer, a massive jolt electrified his entire body, so intense and complete was the massive searing pain now coursing through him that any attempt at screaming again wasn't even an option.

His voice failed him and the air inside his body seemingly extracted itself in an instant.

All he found he could do was drop his head down to his chest and inspect with sheer, complete and utter horror at the damage that bestow his eyes as without any ability for his brain to fully comprehend what had actually happened his eyes saw the truth.

This psychopath, had teased him within an infinite level of complete gratification and yet sliced of his entire manhood, right at the base where it connected to his bladder. Blood, urine and semen mixed in a cacophony of excitement and defecating horror, out and down into the awaiting bucket below.

Incapable of accepting this horror to himself Terrance watched the man, place his manhood into the jar with his awaiting nipples.

Then, having placed a lid upon the jar turned one last time, walked back to Terrance, brandishing an office stapler. He pulled the photos from out of his pocket and stapled them to Terrance's chest, followed by his hands for one last desperate viewing before his body would, at some point, ultimately give up.

Chapter 5

Adrian sat with his feet up on the sofa, coffee in hand, TV remote in the other, flicking between the documentary channels. Monica was off on her way to work, she had been putting in as much overtime as she could, they could do with the money after all, Adrian wasn't able to get overtime as his job doesn't offer it, so this sunny weekend sees Monica at work and Adrian idly scanning the cable TV.

Monica bendt down to the sofa and kissed Adrian who reciprocated, playfully pulling her onto the sofa with him. Giggling, Monica gave Adrian a gentle slap before returning to her feet and calling "Bye darling, love you" as she left, the door banging shut with a happy kind of authority as she closed it behind her.

Adrian returned to the TV. The weekend didn't seem wonderfully interesting, documentaries, pawn shows, auction shows, pickers, loggers or fishermen. It was endless reality TV documentaries.

What he wanted was nature, mystery, horror. A commercial comes on the TV advertising a show about clearing buildings, warehouses, properties, including homes and suddenly Adrian's mind begins to drift back to the empty flat in their building. It had been weeks, maybe even longer since he had spoken to the builders about it.

Adrian sat there, contemplating what might have happened, why they may have left so suddenly. Was it as simple as non payment of rent? Or was there something more to it? He mulled it over in his mind, all the possibilities, it seemed endless.

Then gradually it began to dawn on him that they hadn't seen their neighbour in a few days either. Adrian usually bumped into him on his way out or upon his return. But he hadn't seen him for a little while. Was it a few days, a week, fortnight, hell he wasn't sure when it was that he had last seen him, let alone actually spoken to him. Is he on holiday? Probably.

But Adrian's gut didn't feel right. It felt weird, horrible in fact, it seemed to be screaming out to him that something was right about this, that there was definitely something very wrong. Problem was he couldn't prove anything was actually wrong. He could hardly call the police and tell them that two people were missing although he didn't actually know them, didn't see them leave and didn't see anything weird or untoward happen.

They would laugh and tell him to go away. No, he was going to have to have a nose around, talk to people, ask about, see what other people thought.

First he thought, let's have a look next door. 27 was directly opposite their flat, so if something had happened, how the hell did neither of them nor the people at number 28 heard let alone seen anything? That's what bothered him. He could accept that they had gone away or left suddenly, but they hadn't heard anything.

Whether something bad had occurred or not, the fact that they hadn't heard anything at all is what really troubled Adrian.

Adrian decided he had to do something so making out that they needed milk and odd things from the shop he left hoping that he would bump into his neighbour, be that either number 28 or number 27 themselves. So off he went to the shop.

About an hour later and laden with a small feast of milk, snacks and nibbles, Adrian returned. And as luck should have it, their neighbour, from number 28 was just leaving. Adrian wasted no time and set about finding out. Both greeting each other with warm smiles, Adrian pretended to act casual about the subject as though it wasn't something that overly concerned him, even though it did, it grated on him all the time now.

"Here, you haven't heard or seen anything of them have you?" Adrian quizzed.

“No mate, not for ages. Think they may have moved, mind you I didn't hear them go, must have been bloody quiet.”

The man, young, in his mid twenties and with a friendly if unkempt face, laughed. Adrian followed suit and pretended. The young man said his farewells and left, tapping Adrian on the arm, holding it there slightly for a second or two as he left.

This information made Adrian feel even more unsettled now. He had hoped to have what he still felt were silly unfounded fears of an overactive imagination quashed on the spot. Instead they seemed to be confirmed to him.

This was number 2 and no-one had heard anything of either of them. How many more had there been that nobody noticed, or even cared about for that matter? He had to know. Putting his little bag of shopping away indoors, he grabbed his keys once more and decided that he needed to do some snooping.

Pulling a packet of cigarettes out of his pocket, he looked at them for a second before deciding that they were the perfect excuse to be wandering around. He was simply having a cigarette. After all they were banned from inside all public buildings now, and Monica would have no stock with smoking in the flat, so he had to smoke outside.

Lighting up a cigarette as he exited the main security door, one of the neighbours from the level below them came past. “Hello Adrian, Monica still not letting you smoke indoors then?” She asked, a gentle smile flowing across her face.

“No. no way” Adrian replied, releasing a small nervous chuff
as he did so.

“Good for her. Got to keep you boys under control or all chaos breaks loose.” Again she laughed, her greetings said she moved on inside the building to her own flat.

Adrian began to walk around the outside of the building. He knew he hadn't and wasn't doing anything wrong but he still didn't want to be seen by that caretaker. There was something off about him.

Adrian couldn't figure it out. He still hadn't met him or even seen him yet, but even so, he gave him the willies. The fact that he was yet to meet him in person as such was part of it, and yet there was something else about him that meant that he just gave Adrian the creeps.

This was one weird, maybe creepy was the right word after all, dude. Adrian continued walking around, pretending he was just there strolling as he smoked, but all the while subtly looking for any tell tale signs of something wrong, something to back up his feelings that the two men's disappearances was in fact suspicious. He didn't really know what he was looking for, but had to look any way. It felt like he was supposed to.

It wasn't long until he started to notice things that seemed not quite right. First, there was a shoe, a single shoe, lying on its side, next to the curb. Why one shoe? He thought. Two was understandable, someone didn't want them any more, being lazy or dirty scumbags, dumped them in the road or on the path and thus they end up by the curb, but one shoe, that's just weird.

But as he continued, he noticed what looked like bloody smears on a piece of white wall. Not just one. but three smears, almost like fingers. Had someone been hurt? Really? This was getting somewhat unnerving now, Adrian thought to himself.

He finished off his cigarette and made his way inside through the rear security door using his key fob to unlock the door. He looked over to his left at the lifts and in a fit of unusual health consciousness, he decided to take to the stairs. Again, each flight he climbed, he noticed a smear, a drop or a speck of what looked like blood.

This wasn't right. A caretaker that didn't clear that up? Was it fresh? Something wasn't right, no something wasn't right at all and Adrian began to pick up his pace, his gut was beginning to twist and knot with nerves and he didn't want to be on the stairs here when the caretaker came. He creeped him out and Adrian was sure that he was involved somehow. Suddenly Adrian heard a door somewhere above him, swing open and with a clunk, shut tight again.

He continued walking on a bit but got that eerie feeling like he wasn't alone. Hesitantly, he looked up. There not more than maybe half a dozen floors above him, a pair of piercing, evil looking eyes looked down at him, burning through him with suspicion and with cold acknowledgement.

Adrian could sense it, the "I know what you have been doing. I know what you are up to." This felt like danger, *real* danger.

Adrian began to run up the stairs hoping that this man, this creepy, dark, horrible looking figure didn't get to him before he got to his own floor and behind his own front door.

Running faster and faster, now leaping one, two even a third step, pulling himself up using the handrail, Adrian made it to his landing and burst through the door just as he could hear the caretaker get to the floor behind him. This was too close. Way too close.

He fumbled for his keys out of his pocket before managing to scramble the front door key into the lock first time. Well that never happens in the movies, Adrian thought.

Flinging the door open, he rushed inside and turned around to see the caretaker stroll onto his landing just as he slammed the door closed.

Adrian ran into the kitchen, poured himself a drink and slumped down into the sofa, his breath heavy, panting as his heart continued to race. Before he knew it the lock clicked in the door. Adrian's heart raced once more, a terror flushed through him, could it be him? Surely not. He couldn't have a key to his flat could he?

It was a stupid thought, but still the lock was turning and someone was trying to gain access and he wasn't sure that it wasn't this creepy man.

Eventually the lock gave and the door opened. Adrian jumped and curled into the corner of the sofa, unable to find a secure place to hide in time without being caught by this person that has made it clear that he is now on their hit list.

The clunk of each step as the person walked through the corridor, that they had yet to get carpeted, made his heart race ever faster, surely he couldn't take any more without dying of a heart attack.

He closed his eyes, convinced that his tormentor had come to dispose of him for his curiosity.

The waft of fresh air was impossible to ignore, Adrian screwed his eyes closed and balled his fists. If he was going down, at least he would get a few hits in first. He felt that waft of air closer than ever, no more than a few inches from his head.

“Adrian, what they hell are you doing?”

That wasn't the voice of a large, creepy potential serial killer. He opened his eyes and there before him was the most beautiful sight. That of his Monica, his beautiful Monica, back from work. Not *him*. The relief was unmistakable and he immediately un-clenched his hands and exhaled deeply and loudly.

“Thank god. I thought it was......”

Adrian pulled back.

He hadn't said anything about any of this before and now here he was going to unburden himself with what had happened and what he thought, all of a sudden, just as Monica had arrived home from work? He decided it was best not to and let the conclusion to the sentence go missing, floating away in the unsaid.

“What?” Monica quizzed smiling, but slightly confused.

“Uh, nothing, it doesn't matter, babe.” Adrian replied, feeling a little silly. But he knew what he felt, he knew something was going on and he knew he hadn't imagined or hallucinated being followed, chased down even, by that creepy caretaker.

Adrian and Monica curled up together on the sofa after dinner watching TV. Flicking through the usual bombardment of crap TV, X-factor, Strictly Come dancing, Big Brother, I'm a celebrity and the rest.

Finally they settled on watching an obscure movie channel. Monica lay curled against Adrian, with her head against his shoulder and her hand gently across his chest. She could feel him breathe, she could almost feel like she could hear it, hollow and apprehensive.

“Are you alright darling?” Monica said, leaning up a little, raising her head, but retaining her hand upon his chest.

“Yeah, I'm fine.” Adrian said, uncharacteristically short. “Really?” Monica pressed.

“Yeah, sure.” Again came his somewhat terse response.

“Now you see, I don't believe you. You never answer or speak like this. Something's bothering you. So tell me, what is it?” Monica argued, taking control unequivocally.

“You really want to know?” Adrian asked. Monica nodded.

“Alright, but if you tell me I'm being stupid, imagining things or anything, then.....”

“I won't, I promise.” Monica broke in.

“Alright” Adrian continued. “I know how it sounds but trust me. There is something going on in here. This building I mean”

“Like what?” Monica quizzed.

“I don't know exactly but I'm telling you something ain't right here. After the day today, I'm convinced there is some bad shit going on.”

“What do you mean?” Monica narrowed her eyes, intrigued but somewhat suspicious of what she was hearing. It wasn't like Adrian hadn't pulled a stupid prank or an idiotic stunt to scare her before.

“I mean some real messed up shit. Look, think about it this way. First we hear that someone has done a bunk from one of the other flats right?” Adrian began explaining.

“Yeah, nothing strange with that.” Monica argued.

“No, but the guy doing the clearing said nobody knew where they had gone and they were told to clear as a void, but he has a friend inside the council who had said that they hadn't owed any rent, they weren't in debt.” Adrian began to get animated as he spoke.

“So” Monica replied shrugging her shoulders.

“So, it means they had no reason to do a bunk. Now, know the bloke opposite us?”

“What, number 27?” Monica asked making sure she was keeping up with Adrian's increasing excited thought process.

“Yeah, well have you seen him lately?” Monica thought for a second. Then shook her head.

“Nor have I, nor has 28 and nor have the other 2 tenants by the looks of it. And he can't have moved because one of us on this floor would have seen or at least heard him moving his stuff out. But nobody has.”

“What? You think he's dead in there?” Monica frowned at the thought as she spoke it.

Adrian tilted his head in a quizzical gesture. “Either that, or something has happened to him or been *done* to him.”

“Oh come on Ade, you can't be serious, really? You must be.....” Monica tailed off before she said it. Then continued with a different comment.

“Look, I'm sure whatever has gone on is perfectly normal, nothing to worry about. It's good that you are taking an interest in looking out for our neighbours, but it sounds like you are over thinking this a bit. With good intentions, don't get me wrong, but....”

“I know what you are trying to get at babe, believe me, I thought it myself. But ever since we got here, something just hasn't felt right. Just something, I don't know, something not good, something......sick.”

Adrian paused for a moment and took a few deep breaths. Monica could see he was getting worked up and decided not to say anything and left him to continue what he had to say in his own time.

“Take today. That shit is totally messed up. I went downstairs for a ciggie right? Your mate comes in says hello, I decide to have a walk around round while I have a smoke. That's when I see what looks like, no, what *really* looked like blood, on the path and smeared on the wall. I walked further round to the back door, right? Still, drops & smears everywhere. So I finished my cigarette, getting edgy, I, for whatever reason just bolt up the stairs. I mean, it's a fucking long walk up here, but, I still ran up them. Until I get half way, then a door goes above me. I look up & it's him.” Adrian said. His voice now breathy.

“Who?” Monica asks, now intrigued.

“The caretaker. Creepy fucking dude.” Adrian says.

“So?”

“So? So, he stares down right at me. No, fuck that, he stared right through me, Mon, right into me like he was sizing me up for something. I mean if he wanted a fight, I'd have given him one, but it wasn't that. He looked like he wanted more than that. Something bad. I start to bolt again, and that's when he *chases* me. Down the stairs and on to the landing. That shit was messed up. I ran in and slammed the door. Haven't looked out since. I was sitting here wondering if he'd try to break in or not. Then I thought about you. I was worried he'd take you too. I mean, I got a glimpse as he walked on to the landing and I noticed he was carrying something in his hands, but whatever it was, I'm pretty damn sure it had blood on it.”

“Oh baby. Look, whatever happened, I'm sure it was....”. Monica tried reassuring him.

“Look, I know how it sounds. I mean it's been running through my head for hours. But trust me. There is something really messed up about this place and that bloke. I really think he has had something to do with those people going missing.”

“Look, babe, I know you wouldn't go this far to scare me, right?” Monica began to respond.

“You think I am pissing about with you?” Adrian jumped in.

“No, but listen for a second, it's not like you haven't done some messed up jokes before.” Monica explained.

“Oh, nice. So I do a few risky jokes, now I'm the fucking boy who cried wolf? Just waiting to drop one on you and shout boo? Fuck you! I'm not pissing about. I'm telling you. There is some messed up shit going on and now some sick fuck is after me. We need to do something or get the fuck right out of here. 'Cos, I'm telling you, it ain't safe here now. Not for either of us, but especially me. This fucker is not going to stop.”

“I thought you said you could take him on.” Monica said, the mocking tone in her voice louder than she intended.

“I would, but he ain't just a creepy fucker, he's a creepy fucker with sharp stuff and he knows where to go to hide.” Adrian said animatedly.

“OK, suppose it's true, go double lock the door and put the chain on while I go run you a bath and make a drink. You're stressed out and could do with a nice long soak in a hot bath. I'm sure you'll feel better afterwards and let's deal with it tomorrow, OK? I mean, it's not like he can do anything about it now nor we until the morning. Alright?”

Adrian reluctantly agreed, nodding his head.

Chapter 6 – Revealing.

Adrian awoke feeling somewhat refreshed. He still knew something was wrong with the place but he had to go back to work, he couldn't very well hide out here to solve a mystery that he couldn't prove existed and most wouldn't believe even occurred. He turned over in the bed and looked at Monica, he had forgotten quite how beautiful she looked as she slept there silently. His snow white, he called her.

"Because you are the most beautiful woman I have ever seen and you always sleep so quietly" he had explained one day, when she had asked him why he would call her it.

Kissing her on the cheek, she smiled gently and carried on sleeping as he rose himself and began to get dressed.

Slipping out of the room quietly, he freshened up in the bathroom and then grabbed his coat from the stand, his keys off the side and his phone, slipping them into his jacket pockets before closing the door behind him as quietly as he could whilst still ensuring it closed with the reassuring clunk as the latch slipped into place.

Lunch time came and Adrian was feeling better to have been away from the building and back at work. He knew he had to go back, but he had begun to think Monica had been right after all. Maybe he had been overthinking this whole thing. He had let his imagination get the better of him. It was all probably normal enough, it just looked odd because of accidental coincidences, nothing more than that. Another couple of hours and he could be back with Monica, curled up watching some weird sci-fi or horror film on TV.

He hated these months where their days off missed by a day with each other. It was more frustrating than if they were separated by weeks or months.

The figure stands outside the door. Silently, but intently. Slowly they reach forward and knock loudly using the large brass door knocker, shaped like a grotesque. The door opened after a few moments quiet and Monica stood there a few seconds, neither saying anything. Then the figure reached across and took a hold of Monica's arm and pulled her from the door way. The door closing behind her as though an invisible force had willed it so.

Monica let out a gasp, the unfortunate fact being that nobody else on the floor were actually home to witness the scenario take place. The figure led Monica off the floor, out and down the stairs. Down they went, each pause she made led to a sharp dig in the back with something sharp. Most probably a knife of some description. Adrian had been right all along.

Down they went, each flight showing another definite indication of Adrian's telling the truth. Blood splattered along the edges of the walls, dripping down onto the floors and catching on the edges of the steps and even the bars of the handrails. Each stain or little puddle, seemingly telling its own story of suffering.

All at the hands of this terrifying man, figure, creature, whatever *it* was. It certainly wasn't human, no human would do this. Not in brazen daylight without the hope of somebody discovering them.

The journey continued until they reached the bottom of the stairs. Then reaching out the caretaker pulled on Monica's arm once again, dragging her almost, through the set of double doors and out of the rear security door and into the open. Suddenly he stopped and turned to face an old painted white door.

Pulling a set of keys from off of his belt, the caretaker unlocked the door, which then gave with a loud crack and a creak of groaning protest and being opened after what seemed must have been a fair time, maybe years, decades even, Monica considered to herself.

Turning back to Monica, the figure dressed as a caretaker, reached once more and then pushed her forcefully in the back. Monica, with little choice it seemed, complied and walked into the dark, barely lit area. A maze of corridors each with a row of doors, each housing a room of its own for storage.

The only light being a dim light in the corner of where Monica stood. Slowly the figure led her into a wider space. There Monica looked around. Her breath was taken away, not a sound would find its way from her lungs and out. Just stunned silence. She could not believe the horror before her eyes.

Holding the blade, he points it in the direction of a young woman hanging from her wrists by barbed wire. The blood trickling down her arms to her elbows and on to her shoulders. The caretaker looked back to Monica and smiled a sadistic smile. The poor young girl hanging there like a slab of beef at an abattoir.

“What? What the hell has she ever done to merit this? You bastard!” Monica found her voice in one large spurt.

Again the caretaker smiled an evil grin, then held the knife to the girls throat. Monica felt herself twitch with an instinctive reaction to do something to help the poor girl. But the moment she twitched as she went to move, the caretaker pointed the knife directly into Monica's face, the tip of the blade mere centimetres from cutting her. Monica froze once again. The man turned to the doors to their left, two large doors that had sliding bolts locking them in place.

Looking at them, looking back at the girl, deep into her eyes, then back at the doors, the caretaker smiled indecently, moving the knife up to the girls throat once more before letting it slide, in a twisted interpretation of seduction, then with a sudden grasp of her hair, lopped a lock of hair off and placed it on the shelf beside him. Reaching up he released the barb wire restraints and the girl dropped to the floor. Stunned. The three of them stood there in a sort of stalemate, until Monica broke the silence and shouted:

"GO! RUN!"

The girl still unsure what to make of the situation hesitated for a moment or two before realising she at least had half a chance of freedom, scrambled to her feet and bolted barging the doors wide open, revealing a now bright sunny day. The girl rushed out into the street, out into the private roadway and onto the cover of the storm drain.

Her freedom tragically short, the girl's eyes widened with a sickening realisation that she had almost been free but for the path she had willingly trod in her haste to escape.

Slowly she began to sink, lower and lower, as the razor sharp blades of the drainage cover used her own body weight against her, cutting through her feet, dropping her down, then through her legs, every piece of her body that made contact was instantly sliced like a piece of fruit in a blender.

Blood washing out and around the road and running back down the bowl of concrete that encased the drainage cover and down into the storm drain itself. Soon amidst the now gurgling sounds that echoed in Monica's head, all that remained was a head.

Turning back, that disgustingly satisfied expression, unforgettable, burnishing itself into Monica's mind, decorating this madman's face.

Suddenly with a swift swing of his arm, the caretaker landed a deft blow to Monica's face, taking her clean off her feet and into the air a fully couple of inches, before sending her crashing to the ground with a slap and a thud. Her head spun and her vision blurred before going black entirely, the sounds of her immediate world fading into nothing.

Turning to meet the wide open world, the caretaker lifted the grate and kicked the head down into the awaiting hole. Then closing the two doors behind him, bolting them shut, he resumed his attention towards Monica.

Adrian pulled up to the car park and settled in to his usual space. Turning the ignition off, he reached over and pulled out the carrier bag containing store bought *meal for two* take away and a bottle of white wine. With a smile on his face and a determination that he would make up for his stupidity last night, he strolled into the building.

As he got to their floor, he got an eerie feeling. A feeling he had hoped he had pushed aside, pushed away. But here it was again, stronger than ever before. Nervously he walked up to their front door. Unlocking the door, Adrian called out to Monica. But to no reply. Walking inside, Adrian placed the wine and food on the kitchen counter and set about looking through the flat for her.

When it became clear that she wasn't there, he looked for a note to explain where she may have gone. Nothing. Pulling the phone from his pocket, Adrian dialled Monica's number. It rang, and rang and rang. But she did not answer.

Now he knew there was something wrong, she always answered her phone, even if it was those annoying PPI calls, "Just in case" she would always repeat. Grabbing his keys, Adrian rushed back outside to find her. He desperately hoped she had simply gone to the convenience store for something.

Rather than contemplate the idea that she had been taken, by this sicko that pretended to be a caretaker. How was he getting away with it? Adrian thought, surely somebody must know about him, they *must* know. He made his way down to Lindsay's flat, just in case she was there.

“Monica? No hun, I haven't seen her all day. She hasn't been here, sorry darling, if she pops in before you find her, I'll get her to call.”

“Thank you” Adrian replied, knowing for certain now that something bad had happened.

Making his way outside the building, he lit another cigarette, he needed to calm himself, if he was going to do something about it, he needed to be able to think clearly.

He decided that he would leave *no* stone unturned. He would find out where Monica was and deal with this fucker once and for all.

He was up to no good and he would find out what exactly he was up to and make sure the council or whoever he had to go to, got rid of him once and for all.

Walking down the side of the building he noticed some fresh drops of blood. His gut twisted as his skin began to run cold. He pulled his phone out again and rang Monica's phone again. This time he heard it, loud and clear.

It was around here somewhere and it was really close by. Over and over he rang it. Then as he followed the sound, he spotted it, sitting down beside the curb of the pavement.

"What the hell is it doing here" Adrian muttered to himself. Bending down to pick it up, he saw more blood.

"Oh God no.." Adrian proclaimed loudly to himself.

He didn't want to, but he had to check where this blood was leading. He followed it to the storm drain. The thought of it going to a drain, for just a brief second brought some relief, surely it wouldn't be blood if it was going to a storm drain right?

But getting closer he saw something glint off the setting sunlight. Peering down into the cover he saw what looked like an earring shining and reflecting the light from the low sun.

Reassured he looked a bit deeper just as a flow of waste water flowed through the pipe below, turning moving the earring and bobbing it on top of the blood as the head that housed it began to bob up and down and turned over to one side, coming to rest angled directly up towards Adrian's peering face.

Now he saw the full extent of the horror he wished not to think about for days, staring right back at him, eye to lifeless eye.

Adrian backed off in a panic, losing his footing and falling backwards, landing on his backside. Scrambling away from the awful sight he had just witnessed, wishing to all the heavens that it wasn't true, knowing full well what he had just seen with his very own eyes.

Whoever that poor girl was, surely she hadn't deserved that, not one single bit.

Dragging himself along his backside, Adrian pulled himself back onto the curb once more, where he promptly vomited the last remnants of his early lunch into the roadway.

Pulling himself up to his feet, leaning up against the wall, he wiped his mouth with his sleeve, spitting the taste of puke from his mouth with several globs of saliva and phlegm.

Looking up at last after a several minutes, Adrian looked and found himself staring at that wall he had the other day, there were more blood splatters and this time and clear, defined hand mark. Beside the bloody hand mark Adrian realised was a set of double doors.

Looking up there was an old painted metal mesh grill, which showed a faint orangey glow behind it. Clearly there was a light in there, even if it was evidently quite ancient given its dim hue.

He began scanning for ways inside. There was a gap, maybe if he rattled it enough, the lock would break or give enough for him to open one of the doors. As he shook the doors he could hear the distinctive rattle of a bolt on the other side.

If he could only make it move enough it would fall out of its position and drop down, giving him an opportunity to squeeze himself inside.

Finally the bolt did indeed drop, but the door was still secure enough not to afford Adrian a way inside.

He settled for the realisation that he would have to break in, so pulling as hard as he could, eventually the old wood began to splinter and pull away from the bolted locks. With a load crack and the sound of wood splintering the door suddenly gave way and Adrian made his way inside the strange area.

A rush of a sick inducing stench of rotting meat, urine and shit, mostly human, he determined, hit Adrian in the face. It was all he could do not to lose what was left inside his stomach again.

Walking through, it was like a labyrinth. Corridors in all directions with multiple doors along them. Adrian picked a corridor and began walking down it.

Opening the first door, he leapt back, even in the dim light of this stinking hell hole of a place, he could see the half dismembered corpse of another unlucky victim.

Then next door, another, mutilated in yet another god forsaken way. Again and again, Adrian discovered body after body, hanging up by chains, rope, wire, cables, hooks, or in one case, impaled upon a what looked like a sharpened metal bollard which had been cemented into the ground.

The sights were too horrible to imagine, let alone describe to the police, if he ever got out of here alive. He hoped to god that Monica wasn't here and that he got out alive himself to report this real life horror movie scene.

As Adrian turned the corner the light got slightly better and this time we was afforded a better look around where he stood. Only for to wish he hadn't, if it was possible, the scene had gotten even worse.

To the right of him was a selection of shelving, each showcasing a selection of jars. Each proudly displaying a human body part, and some displaying things he couldn't even imagine what they were. He kept looking around but Adrian got the definite feeling that he needed to get out right now.

He turned to find the exit and bumped into something soft, but fresh feeling, untainted or defiled even. Looking up he was greeted by the sight that instantly brought all his emotions to the fore in a flood of tears that flowed easy and freely down his face.

"NO! NO, NO, NO, NO, NOOO!!!!" Adrian cried loudly.

There hanging by nylon rope was his sweetheart Monica, the one person that had understood him better than anyone else. The one person who had stuck by him and supported him no matter what, even when everybody else had walked away from him.

Hanging like a useless piece of meat, ready for the slaughterhouse. No, dead or not, he wasn't going to let that happen to his beautiful Monica.

Suddenly Adrian heard a door go somewhere in this place. It wasn't where he had come from, he thought, but somewhere else. Damn it, there were more than one way in *and* out of this place. Although this increased their odds of getting out safely, it also reduced their odds of sneaking out without being found.

They may now have a 50-50 chance of getting out without encountering the psycho, it also meant they had a 50-50 chance of being trapped at either end, no matter which way they went. Now he could hear the clunking footsteps drawing closer.

Adrian stopped and held his breath. He looked at Monica, trying to figure out a way to get her down and escape without being discovered or trapped.

Just at that moment, Monica opened her eyes and looked down blankly at Adrian. Adrian's face lit up knowing she was alive, even if it was barely.

It was then that he smelt the unmistakable odour of that uniform of the caretaker. A mixture of cleaning fluids, polish, refuse and that was it, that was the smell he couldn't place all that time ago, the smell of rotting human flesh.

This sick had been doing this for years undetected, somehow, lord knows how but right now Adrian knew he had to run and try and get Monica in a moment once he had out smarted this crazy bastard killer.

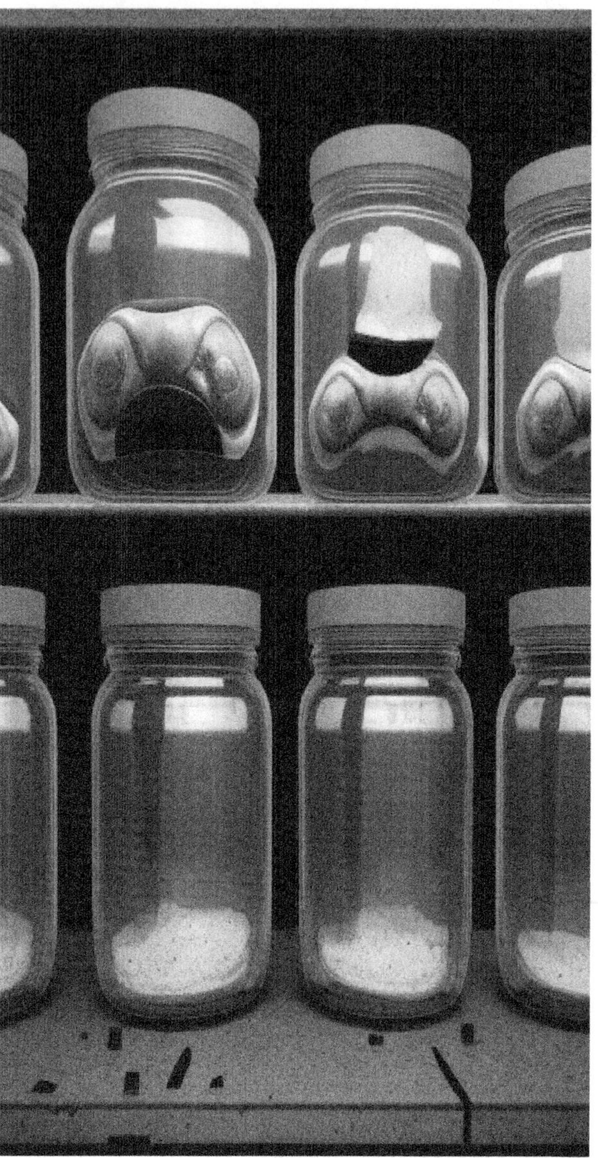

He turned only to come face to face with the killer. Fleet footed he ducked and dodged the swinging hammer laden arm of the caretaker. Taking off running, Adrian ran down the first corridor, pursued by the killer, methodically stalking him.

Around and around they went down corridor after corridor, Adrian sprinting as fast as he dare without being able to see exactly where he was going, all the while the caretaker pursued him, hunting him down like a predator to its prey. Waiting for it to make a mistake or collapse of exhaustion.

Just as Adrian turned one more corner he noticed daylight at the end. A way out at last he thought. At last, he could find someone to help, call the police and catch this monster. Adrian renewed his efforts to escape and raced as fast as his feet would carry him, suddenly he felt himself beginning to lose control, his legs going slightly wobbly, his balance compromised.

As though he were watching a movie on pause, suddenly play, he watched the door suddenly slam shut, his heart sank and just as he attempted to stop himself, he heard first of all, the awful sound of a bang, his mind not registering quite what had happened, let alone what going on.

Then Adrian felt his feet leave the ground, he went to look down, only for his mind to finally absorb the full scale of what had just happened when he realised he couldn't look down, realising that in fact he had been swept off of his feet by a swing hook attached to the ceiling.

He hadn't noticed it when he had entered the place, but right now it was all too painfully obvious as he swung from it, as it hooked him through his throat and up through the lower half of his jaw and out through his mouth.

His voice box and vocal cords destroyed, there was no point in trying to scream for help, instead the tears flowed down his face once more, at the all the dead, the lives lost, the senseless murder, the pain and his lost hope of rescuing his beloved Monica.

He hung there, desperate and pathetic for a few moments until he felt the pressure lift from his face and head. A large muscular arm wrenched him up and off of the hook, but Adrian knew who it was and knew that this wasn't hope, this was the next stage in his damnation.

The Caretaker swung him across the corridor and into a door, which promptly broke, showering Adrian with dust and splinters. Adrian half dazed crawled in a desperate bid to wake up a last spark of fight in his breaking and pain ravaged body.

With a wild swing with his right leg into open air, he eventually felt a connection and heard a crack and a yelp of pain. He had connected, he had hurt this bastard.

Adrian crawled and slithered his way down the corridor, the orange glow getting brighter again, before long he found himself back where the fight had begun. Staring up again at Monica, strung up like an angel on a cross. He pulled himself up to his feet again, holding on to the shelves for support.

Just then he felt the same familiar grasp and again he was back in the grip of the killer. Now in a choke hold, with his arm around Adrian's neck, he gripped tighter and tighter. Adrian thrashed desperately trying to find something to beat him off for even just a second. Sweeping along the shelf he pushed jars of testes, eye balls, and a human penis, crashing to the ground, the contents, spilling out onto the dirty, dusty floor.

With a growl the monster of a man, gripped tighter. Suddenly Adrian felt his fingers grasp a cable, gripping it, he pulled it towards himself, bring with it an old radio player.

Grabbing the radio he swung it with all of his strength, smashing it deep into the face of his attacker. The impact causing both the caretaker to reel backward and stumble and the radio to spark into life.

The radio dropping from Adrian's hand hung in mid air swinging by the power cable as it played The Statler brothers “I'll go to my grave, loving you....”

The song was haunting Adrian much like this crazed psychopath. The respite was to be brief though and with a sudden rush of fire like pain, intense and incredible shooting through his body he realised that the caretaker had buried a knife deep into his back, Adrian slowly slumping back to the ground.

All sound began to fade into the background leaving just the sight of Monica hanging there above him and the radio continuing to serenade him in his final moments.

With a desperate prayer he mouthed the words to the only prayers he knew, looking deep into the eyes of his beloved. Suddenly her head drops down almost to meet his gaze directly. Then with an easy tug, Monica freed her hands from their bindings and she dropped casually to the ground.

She walked over and stood in front of Adrian's prone body. The caretaker looked down at him, then looked up at Monica before stapling photographs of Adrian, taken of him.

Taken at the funeral of what he had always said was his best friend. Adrian had always played the dutiful friend who was torn apart by the early, unfortunate death of his best friend. The other pictures were on different occasions, of him chasing his best friend, some with open arms and hands, others with him carrying bats, even one with a knife, even though it looked fake.

But most of all, the poor lad looked terrified, while Adrian and his friends look positively maniacal and sadistic in their glee chasing him.

This was the same lad that had killed himself, stating how he “couldn't take it any more.” At the time he had made it sound to her, the same way it had sounded to everyone, that he had committed suicide because, sadly he had problems with life that he just couldn't seemingly overcome.

How that now took new precedence. How she saw it for what it actually was now. Leaning down she kissed Adrian on the lips, his eyes covered in tears of fear, despair and broken hope. But Monica could now only see the hate that boiled from behind his guilty pleas of hope.

Monica took a knife from her belt and drove it deep into Adrian's chest, fresh *guilty* blood pumped out with vigour, Adrian's eyes began to glaze and before long had faded out to an almost colourless fog as the life he had clung to so desperately let go of him and leaked out onto the blade of Monica's knife.

With that done, Monica turned to the caretaker, whose face was oozing blood and a hole was clearly visible to his forehead. She looked at him, looking back up at her, from down on his knees, that sinister smile still as strong as ever, only now it was smeared with his own blood, running down his face and down into his mouth, covering his sharp fang-like teeth.

With that sight in her mind Monica turned, looked around and noticed the sharpened floor scraper leaning against a wall. Reaching over, she grabbed it, walked around and stood behind the grinning, killer caretaker.

Raising the weapon up in the air like a giant stake, she brought it down like a guillotine, down onto his neck, blood spraying out everywhere, spraying across her t-shirt and up her own face.

Again she drove it down, over and over until the killer's head plopped off and rolled to a stop against Adrian's leg.

Dropping the floor scraper and looking down at the fallen bodies of her lover and the killer he had warned her of, she heard a bleep, a familiar message tone. It was the same one her mobile phone made. Looking down she saw the screen of her phone poking out from Adrian's trouser pocket. Picking it up, Monica inspected the screen. One message from "Unknown". She left it and placed it in her pocket before casually picking up the head of the killer, looking deep into it's now strangely widened eyes, she carried it by the hair and placed it on to the shelf beside the jars of other body parts.

Retrieving the keys from the caretaker's body, she left. jamming the doors closed and slid the keys minus one specific key, beneath the caretaker's door, before returning home.

Promptly stripping off her clothes as she got in and closed the door, putting them in the wash basket. Monica run the water and soaked in the luxury of a steaming hot bath. Once clean of all the death upon her, Monica dried herself and got dressed.

Just then she remembered the the message on her phone. Retrieving it from her jeans, she looked at the screen, before pressing it and revealing the message. "#18 ADULTERY." And that was all. Number 18? That was her best friend. Her ever helpful best friend of a few floors down, Lindsay. Monica thought for a moment. Suddenly all those little innocent situations played themselves out like dirty little movies inside her head.

She kept looking in disbelief. But her mind began to run through all those little innocent situations over and over again. Like Lindsay, offering to help when they had moved in. All those little touches she had made to Adrian's arms, stroking them even.

How cosy they had looked, giggling together, whenever she had come back into the room after making tea and dinner and the pair trying to separate, create a distance between each other, pretending nothing had happened, trying to hide what was indeed going on.

How they had often suddenly stopped as she entered the room again, hushing themselves like they had a dirty little secret, just the two of them and she had almost caught them out. Well now she realised they did. And she had. She just hadn't wanted to believe it. There were more occasions where she'd had reason enough to question but chosen not to.

Her hand going white as she gripped the phone ever tighter, she snapped out of her trance like state of remembrance, broke her grip and looked back down at it, finally pressing delete.

The screen went blank, Monica threw the phone on to the bed and put fresh make up on. Suddenly the house phone rang.

Answering it cautiously Monica listened for the mysterious callers reply. “Hello, Mon? Oh thank god. Ade was here a while ago looking for you, he looked awful, he was almost crying, saying he couldn't find you and was going out to track you down. Did...did he find you? I mean, did you meet up eventually?” Lindsay stammered out excitedly.

“Oh yes, fine, no problem, don't worry hun.” Monica answered rather coldly.

"Oh, uh, good, I mean that's great. Thank god. I was worrying sick, I kept ringing your number but it wouldn't go through, then I tried your home number, finally you answered after about the hundredth time. Nothing bad has happened has it?" Lindsay continued to rush out the words like they were going out of fashion.

"Oh no. Well, we got into an argument Lin, I found out he was cheating on me and I told him to pick. Them or me. So he took off." Monica explained. Her improvisation impressed even herself.

"Oh. Oh no, I'm sorry hun. Oh babe. Come down, we'll have some wine, put on some glad rags, I got some gorgeous ones you just *need* to try on and we'll disappear for a good old girls only night out eh?"

"That sounds perfect *hun*" Monica replied, accentuating the "hun" with an exaggerated manner. Not that Lindsay picked up on it at all.

“That sounds perfect, I'll be right down” Monica continued.

Hanging up she walked into the kitchen and picked up the bottle of wine, before leaving the flat. Knocking on Lindsay's door

Monica walked straight in, handing a bottle of wine to her best friend.

A large carving knife, poking out from her jean belt, which glinted, menacingly in the glare of the light behind her.

Printed in Great Britain
by Amazon

46080762R00069